JUNO'S ARK

April 23

Fruitful
PUBLICATIONS

This first edition first published in 2023 by Fruitful Publications

Text and illustrations © 2023 Jim Mellon

Fruitful Publications Limited (t/a Fruitful Publications), English company number 09314658.

For customer service and for information about how to apply for permission to use any copyright material in this book (including permission to reproduce extracts in other published works) please email orders@fruitfulpublications.com or see www.junosark.com

A catalogue record of this book is available from the British Library.

Printed and bound in Great Britain by Micropress

ISBN: 9781739250508

JUNO'S ARK

JIM MELLON

ILLUSTRATED BY SIMONE FUMAGALLI

Contents

1. Don't Be a Chicken, Juno!   7

2. The Big Adventure Begins - Juno is on the Case!   20

3. Free as a Bird!   34

4. Holy Cow, Juno!   50

5. Juno and Team Hoof It to the Cows   59

6. Happy as a Muddy Piggy   80

7. This Little Piggy Won't Go to Market   86

8. The Shiny Spoons of Happiness   103

JUNIPER

JINGLES

JUNO

CHAPTER ONE

Don't Be a Chicken, Juno!

Juno lives in a big house on an island with her sisters, Jingles and Juniper, and their human family. She loves to feel the grass underneath her feet and to sniff exciting smells, so she often explores the forests and fields that surround her. Big because she can stand tall on her hind legs, but thin from all her bouncing around, her slender frame means she can jump high and travel even further.

Jingles likes to join Juno on her expeditions, but she is not as tall or fast so sometimes can't keep up. Juniper, a bit older than her sisters, doesn't like going far from her favourite sofa. When she was a puppy, one of her hind legs got caught in a fence and she was badly injured. The humans made her a wheeled contraption so that she can walk and even run a little bit, but it is not very convenient for joining Juno on her adventures.

One night, when the rest of the house was sound asleep, Juno woke up with a little sneeze. She always woke with a bit of a tingle in her long snout, whether she was waking from a nap or a deep sleep.

There was a loud squawking noise outside, and it sounded like it might be coming from the chicken coop, just a little bit up the hill from the house. It must have been very loud indeed to wake up Juno!

She walked to the back of the kitchen as softly as possible so she didn't disturb the humans and her siblings, then let herself out by jumping up and lifting the latch on the back door (something she had learnt to do when she was a pup). It was still dark outside as she padded up the grassy hill to the coop, which was buzzing with commotion. The air was misty, and Juno could feel the dew underneath her paws.

She had been wary of the chickens when she first met them, as their beaks were sharp and they liked to peck. The chickens in turn had been wary of Juno's size and big teeth. But they had since become good friends, and Juno is particularly close to the Head Chicken, Gladys, who, like her, has Serious Responsibilities. Juno is the Top Dog in her pack of three, and Gladys looks after ten other chickens. All of them had been rescued by Juno's humans when they were small chicks, but Juno didn't know what from. Gladys doesn't like to talk about the past.

Juno saw immediately that something was different in the coop. There were TWELVE chickens. Gladys introduced Juno to the new chicken.

'I've called her Julia,' explained Gladys. 'She didn't even have a name.'

Juno took in the newcomer. One of Julia's wings was badly broken, flapping uselessly at her side. While Gladys' feathers were shiny and healthy, Julia's feathers were covered in dust, and she let out an occasional squawk that seemed to shake her whole body.

'You're in a bad way,' Juno said softly. 'What happened to you?'

'Julia has come from a Bad Place,' Gladys told Juno. 'Nasty humans held her and many other hens hostage in a small cage. They had no room to flap or even turn around. Imagine! No flapping. No sunshine. They are made to lay eggs all the time, even if they don't want to.'

Noticing Juno, Julia's squawking became even louder, and Gladys soothed her by making a funny clucking sound from the back of her throat.

SQUAWK!

'Juno is a friend,' Gladys explained to the frightened bird. 'Can you tell her how you escaped?'

Julia, through shivering and squawks, told the Top Dog her story.

'It was a crow,' she began. 'The one called Charles.'

Charles, a friend of Juno and Gladys', liked to patrol the island from the sky, and on one of his expeditions he spotted a big shed he'd never seen before. As he got closer, he heard the same squawking that Juno had heard, but hundreds and hundreds of squawks all at the same time. He peered through a hole in the roof and saw that it was full of metal cages, all containing chickens, all of them squawking just like Julia. The noise made Charles' ears ring.

'Then Charles came inside,' said Julia, letting out another squawk she couldn't control, 'and he spoke to us until he was chased away by the big round farmer. He told us about life outside the shed.'

That evening, around teatime, he came back. This time, the door to the shed was open, but the cages were shut tight, with only room for him to get his beak through and no more.

Apart from Julia's.

Julia's cage had a small hole in the wire. It was not big enough for Julia, but Charles could almost squeeze through. Almost. He used his strong beak to bend back the wire and make the small hole big enough to squeeze through if he held his breath, then bigger and bigger, until he was finally able to lead Julia out of the cage and through the open door of the shed to freedom.

Charles asked Julia to wait outside behind a tree, while he checked the other cages. They were firmly shut, rescuing the other chickens would have to wait while he got Julia to safety. He remembered Gladys and the humans who looked after her. They surely wouldn't mind one more chicken.

Chickens are not very good at flying, and Julia had a damaged wing, so it took all that night for Charles to get her to the bottom of the hill where Gladys lived, a journey that Juno could do in an hour. Julia hadn't walked very far before as she had been trapped in a cage all her life, so Charles coaxed and encouraged her to take every step. When that stopped working he nuzzled her head and stared up the hill towards the chicken coop. How would he get Julia up there?

He was thinking so hard he didn't notice one of Juno's humans, the lady, come up behind him. It was time to feed Gladys and her flock.

'Then the human picked me up and put me in here with Gladys,' Julia finished.

'How awful!' barked Juno. Julia flinched. 'Sorry,'

the big dog apologised. 'What about the other chickens? We can't leave them there.'

'What can we do?' asked Gladys. 'Charles' beak is much sharper than ours, and it would take us days to reach Julia's farm.' Gladys, thought Juno, was not a brave chicken.

'My teeth are big and sharp,' suggested Juno, 'and I can travel very far. Perhaps I can bend holes in the wire cages just like Charles.'

For the first time, Julia smiled. Her friends might be saved by this big brown dog!

It was settled. Juno would leave as soon as she had her breakfast and bring the chickens back here. Gladys said she quite fancied a bigger flock, and that her humans probably wouldn't mind a few extra chickens to feed. Someone had to stay and make sure the house and its surroundings were safe, and Jingles has a big, deep bark, so Juno left her in charge. Juno licked her paws for luck, said goodbye to her sisters, and bounded out the door.

CHAPTER 2

The Big Adventure Begins -
Juno is on the Case!

Juno dashed down the hill, neglecting to say her
customary "Good Morning" to James the Cat. She
had a special route she took from the house, one
that avoided traffic and trouble. She wasn't sure

what she was looking for – only that it was a big, dark shed with lots of chickens.

Juno already knew the sheep that grazed at the bottom of her hill, though she didn't get on with the Lead Sheep, Ovinius, as well as she did with Gladys.

'Ovinius,' she began, 'have you ever heard of a big, dark building with lots of chickens in it?'

'Yes, of course I have', he said, looking down his long nose at Juno. Well, as down as he could manage, as Juno was rather tall. 'How is it inside the house, Juno?' he asked. 'Do you sleep well in your comfy bed? I used to sleep there once. By the fire, where it was warm.' Ovinius had lived in the house for a while when he was a lamb and had never forgotten it.

'I do like my basket,' Juno replied carefully.
'I'm in a hurry, could you please tell me where the
chicken shed is?'

He pointed his right hoof towards the woods.
'It's somewhere over there,' he laughed to himself
and smirked a sheepy smirk.

Desperate to find the shed as quickly as
possible, Juno thanked him and trotted into the
trees. She walked for a long time. It got darker and
darker as the trees got closer and closer together.
There were no clear paths to follow.

She remembered Ovinius laughing his
sheepy laugh and just as she was
thinking maybe she should
turn around, the ground
fell away beneath her.
She had fallen
down into a
deep, deep
hole.

'Ouff!' she cried out. The bottom of the hole was covered in leaves. 'I am lucky not to have broken any bones!' she thought as she checked her legs for damage.

While Juno could normally jump over high walls, the top of this hole, she assessed, was much higher than the wall in her humans' garden. How was she going to get out?

Juno is a type of dog called a Podenco, and Podencos are famous for being fine escapologists. She had gotten out of multiple scrapes by jumping extremely high or extremely far. Once, she had even jumped across a river when she didn't want to go home. Her humans had to find a bridge to cross it and get her.

'There must be another way out of this hole,' she thought. 'There is a bit of a ledge halfway up and maybe, just maybe, if I can get to the ledge, I might be able to scramble out'.

She tried to jump onto the ledge, not just once, but four times. By now she was tired and thirsty. She didn't want to be alone in the hole, especially in the dark.

'One, two, three – Jump, Juno!' She was so close, but she couldn't quite reach the top. She sank into the leaves on the ground. What a terrible position to be in, dark and lonely and cold. She missed Jingles, she missed Juniper and she was sure they were missing her. How would they cope without her? They were too short to open the latch on the back door to let themselves out.

Juno started to yelp and whine for help. This is how Julia must have felt, she realised, trapped in her cage for so long. There was barely room for Juno to turn around. She stopped yelping. There was a rustling noise. Someone had come!

'I'm here!' she shouted. 'Down here!'

First one black floppy ear, and then another, and then a bunny head appeared at the top of the hole.

'Juno!' the bunny exclaimed. 'What are you doing down there?'

It was Chester, one of her friends. Where Chester was, Horatio his brother was never far behind. They were known as the Rabbit Brothers.

'Oh no', said Horatio, as he saw the poor dog helpless in the big, deep hole. 'Juno, dear friend. Are you alright?'

'No, I'm not,' Juno whined. 'I'm on an important mission and I'm scared that I won't be able to get out. Can you help me?'

The bunnies huddled together, then told Juno that they had a plan. She was to wait right where she was and they would be back soon.

About 15 minutes later, Juno calculated, about the length of time it took her humans to eat dinner, the bunnies returned with a very thick piece of what looked like string.

Chester told her their plan. The bunnies had got hold of 'rope' from the forest, left over by some humans who had been working there. They would tie one end to a tree, then throw the other end to the bottom of the hole, Juno would grip it tightly with her strong mouth.

'What happens then?' she asked.

'Then you pull on the rope, and pull yourself out,' Chester answered.

'That's so clever, thank you,' Juno complimented the Rabbit Brothers as they disappeared from view to tie the rope round a tree. Being in a forest, there were lots to choose from!

The other end of the rope landed next to Juno with a thump as Chester and Horatio threw it down into the hole. Juno closed her mouth around the thick rope. It was a good biting thickness. She thought, 'here goes', and gradually worked her way up to the top of the hole using her strong teeth and jaw. The sides of the hole had some uneven bits that her paws could grasp now she had the rope to grip. In what seemed like an age, but was actually

only a couple of minutes,
Juno reached the ledge,
and then the top.

She was free! Juno threw down the rope and panted heavily.

'Thank you, thank you!' she told the jubilant Rabbit Brothers, who were doing a little dance that their plan had worked. 'I would never have got out without you. Would you help me rescue some more animals?'

'Are they trapped in a hole too?' asked Chester.

Juno explained that she was looking for a big dark shed where lots of squawking chickens lived in cages without enough room to turn around. 'They never even see the sun!'

'The squawking shed?' Chester said. 'That's full of chickens? We thought it was a monster in there. You're going the wrong way, we'll show you where it is. Not far, about an hour and a half's hopping.'

'Hopping?' Juno asked, looking at her own long legs and then at the rabbits' tiny legs.

Chester looked back steadily and said, '*WE* can run faster than you!' The bunnies raced off and it was all Juno could do to keep up! As the forest got lighter, they began to slow down. They couldn't run as fast as Juno for long!

'Come on,' Juno urged. 'We have to get the chickens out before it gets dark. Otherwise we won't be able to find our way back to my house. Let's go - I've got an idea.'

So, the big brown dog, tail up and whiskers quivering, set off again, this time with two rabbits clinging onto her back. They issued useful instructions like 'turn left at this rock' and 'there's a stream up ahead'. Ovinius hadn't known where he was sending her at all! Juno's tail started to tingle as they got closer to the squawking shed.

After about an hour of hard running for Juno, the shed came into view. It was surrounded by a big fence and there were two big ponds of dark liquid near it.

'That looks horrid,' panted Juno, slowing down. 'And what's that smell?'

'It's from those ponds. Listen!' said Horatio. They stood still and heard the squawking of lots of Julias.

Juno had found the squawking shed.

CHAPTER 3

Free as a Bird!

Juno, Chester and Horatio were now so close to the shed that the smell coming from the ponds was unbearable, and the noise of the chickens deafening. They didn't know whether to put their paws over their ears or their snouts.

'Charles is lucky he can't smell very well,' Juno whispered to the rabbits as she looked for the opening in the shed that the bird had used when he rescued Julia. 'There! A broken panel next to those bins.' It was just about big enough for Juno to squeeze through, if she breathed in. Chester and Horatio bounced through easily.

The shed was brightly lit even though there were no windows, and packed with small cages, each containing one or two chickens. There were at least a hundred cages, so Juno realised there was as many as 150 chickens. Jingles always says Juno is very good at arithmetic.

The chickens squawked even louder as they noticed the big dog and her two companions. Julia had warned them the chickens wouldn't have seen animals like them before as they had been shut up in the shed for nearly all of their lives. Juno asked the rabbits to approach the chickens, as they were much smaller than her.

'Julia sent us!' they tried to tell them, but it was hard to be heard over the squawking.

They could barely hear themselves! 'Julia!' they shouted. 'We know Julia!'

'No Julia!' they squawked.

'The chicken that left here last night!' Horatio persisted.

'Red and brown feathers,' added Chester.
'Broken wing.'

    A chicken close to them stopped squawking.
'B-b-b-b-broken wing? She left l-l-l-last night.
With a b-b-b-b-black bird.'

Juno realised that since Gladys had named Julia, none of these chickens must know her as Julia, or even have names themselves. Gradually the message spread from one chicken to another, and the squawks became quieter and quieter.

'She has come to stay at my house and she would like you all to come too,' explained Juno.

'Will we get names?' asked the chicken who had first recognised Julia.

'When we get you all out of here, we will give you names. For now, you must be quiet and let us help you escape!' Juno begged them.

'What about the farmer?' asked a black chicken. 'He lives nearby. He's very bad. If he catches us he will kick us and break our wings, just like Julia's.'

'Don't squawk, don't make a sound and try not to move until we release you!'

She looked around at the chicken mess and feathers strewn everywhere. Was there anything that could open the cages? It was sheer luck that there had been a hole in Julia's cage.

Chester and Horatio went along the cages,

trying them all, but they were securely shut and there were so many that Juno wouldn't have time to open them all, even with their help.

'It's a shame they can't open their own cages,' said Chester.

'That's it!' Juno leapt up. 'They can free themselves!'

'Then why are we here?' asked Horatio, scratching his head. 'And how can they do that?'

'I will use my teeth and snout to open one or two of the cages, since the latches look similar to the kitchen door at home, and you will use your paws to do the same. Once some of the chickens are free, they can help by using their beaks.'

Chester and Horatio hopped up and down.

'That's so clever, Juno!' Horatio said.

In no time at all, all the chickens would be free, and Juno and the rabbits would guide them back to her house where they would live happily ever after.

Juno prised the latch on the first cage with her teeth. It was hard, but with some perseverance it gave way and the cage fell open. One very frightened and unsteady chicken emerged blinking into the open. Hurray!

However, the bunnies were not so successful. Their paws were not as strong as Juno's teeth, and they were finding it hard to open the cages they had been assigned.

'Juno!' Chester wailed. 'We can't do it. You've opened three and we can't even do this one.'

'Work together,' Juno instructed them. 'Four paws are better than two.'

Juno's tail was tingling and jingling! 'I think we need to hurry up,' she said, moving on to another cage. 'Watch me,' she said to the newly free chicken. 'Then you can do the next one with your beak.'

With a bit of effort and co-ordination, Chester and Horatio working together did what working alone did not, and a bedraggled chicken stepped out of the newly-open cage. This chicken watched her friend open another cage, and managed to free her neighbour before the rabbits had opened a second cage.

'Hey! Their beaks are stronger than our paws,' Horatio told Juno.

More and more chickens were emerging from their tiny prisons, some of them limping as their legs had not had any real exercise in a long time. They suppressed the urge to let out happy squawks, as Juno glared at them to keep them quiet and told them to concentrate on getting their friends out.

Sooner than expected, all the chickens had been freed from their cages, and they were milling

around the shed waiting for Juno
to tell them what to do.

'Of course, these l-l-locks are easier to
open from th-th-the outside,' one of them
said to the Rabbit Brothers. 'Otherwise
w-w-w-we would have done it our-s-s-s-selves.'

'Shh!' hissed Juno. 'We have to leave. There's an
opening over there. We will all go out the same way,
but you have to go one by one and be quiet!'

They all formed a line. This was surprisingly disciplined, because chickens are not known for their obedience. One by one, with Juno nudging some of the stragglers along, and the bunnies waiting for them on the outside of the shed, they got through the opening. All 149 chickens, as Juno had guessed.

Juno scolded a few who were making too much noise, but generally the hens were quiet. Now, to get away from the shed! Juno, Chester and Horatio guided their flock of bewildered chickens along a rarely used path. Chester in the lead, Horatio at the back and Juno scampering

from chicken to chicken, nudging them forwards and onwards.

'I-I-I can't g-g-g-go any-m-m-more,' a brown and red chicken said, stopping abruptly. 'I'm d-d-d-done.'

'M-me too,' agreed another.

'And m-m-me.'

Juno could see the sun low in the sky. 'We can't stop now!' she implored them. 'It's just a little bit further. Julia is waiting for you.'

'Julia?' said the brown and red one. 'I w-w-want that name.'

'I-I-I want to be Julia t-t-t-too,' said another.

'And m-m-me.'

'You can't all be Julia,' protested Horatio.

'Actually,' Juno explained, 'none of you can have a name until you get to my house. The Head Chicken has to name you.'

'O-o-of course. The H-h-h-head chicken must n-name us. Is her name Julia?'

They all began to move. Juno sighed in relief. Through walking, hopping and flapping, they reached the bottom of the hill where Juno's house

was, passing Ovinius in his field with the other sheep.

His big eyes widened at the never-ending line of chickens. Missing feathers, broken wings, half-hearted flapping and an occasional squawk, they filed past him on their way to the coop.

'Just a little bit further, then you get your names,' Chester encouraged them.

The 149 chickens, squawking with excitement, filed up the hill to the coop, where Gladys, Julia, and the other chickens were waiting to welcome them.

Gladys' beak fell open. 'The coop will have to be extended,' she said.

Juno's humans had heard the noise and come to see what was going on. One scratched his head. 'Where on earth have you all come from?' he exclaimed.

Juno gave a happy bark and went around and around in a little circle, just as she always did when she wanted her humans' attention.

'Juno!' the man human said. 'Has this got something to do with you?'

CHAPTER 4

Holy Cow, Juno!

Juno had a very big sleep and a very big breakfast the next day. She wolfed the food down, licking the bowl clean, then slurped all the water. It was time to check on the new chickens.

Gladys was there, fussing over the new members of the flock, and one of the humans was busy, hammer and nails in hand, extending the coop so that the extra chickens would have plenty of room to move around. There was also a lot more food and water for them, which Juno was pleased about. She knew her humans would look after everyone.

Julia was very helpful as she recognised most of the new hens by sight, and indeed, had been thinking up new names for some of them. Lots of them wanted to be called Julia.

'How will we know which Julia we are talking about?' Gladys objected. She suggested starting with the letters of the alphabet and going through them a few times to come up with ideas.

The new chickens were all girls, so they had to think of feminine names. They had started with Arabella, Beryl, Clarice, Donna, and so forth, all the way through the alphabet and now they had to start again as there were so many hens to name.

They would have to go through all the letters several times and not use any name twice. It would not be easy. There was a lot of laughter and squawking at some of the suggestions, and of course, some of the chickens who were being given names they didn't like, made a chickeny fuss, stamping their feet and clucking.

One chicken was to be called Jemima. Juno pointed out that that was a duck's name, not a chicken's! They settled on Jane instead.

Next, Juno took her morning walk down the hill. She had a bone to pick with Ovinius, who had sent her the wrong way. She might have never rescued the chickens – or got out of the hole.

When she got down to the field where the sheep were grazing, she called out, 'Ovinius! Come over here, I want a word with you!'

He trotted over with his head down and his tail between his legs. Juno had never seen him like this before. Normally he looked down his long nose at her, head high.

Before she could say anything, Ovinius shuddered and big wet teardrops rolled down his black and white face.

'I'm sorry,' he said. 'I saw those poor chickens last night and realised that's why you wanted to know where the shed was. I sent you the wrong way, it must have taken much longer to find them. I didn't know they needed rescuing.'

'Ovinius,' Juno said sternly. 'I nearly didn't rescue the chickens, I fell down a hole on the way you sent me and couldn't get out.'

'Oh no!' wailed the sheep. 'I truly am sorry. I didn't know. I only want to help now. I want to be a better sheep. Tell me how to make it up to you. I'll help in any way I can. Anything at all!'

'Do you mean that?'

He blinked his wet eyelashes at her. 'Yes. I just want to help. Those poor chickens!'

'Those poor chickens indeed,' Juno agreed, and told Ovinius what she had seen the day before.

The regretful sheep listened to the story of the big dark shed with the poor chickens forced to live in small cages and produce eggs continuously. He was shocked about the conditions the hens had to live in, the smell and the noise, and felt even more ashamed as he and his fellow sheep lived in a pleasant open field of lush green grass – even if it was a bit cold sometimes and didn't have any pillows.

Ovinius remembered some other unhappy animals he had heard about from the local horse, Walter.

'Walter mentioned some animals who are much

bigger than me and you, Juno, about the same size as the big horse himself. And Walter is very, very big indeed,' said the reformed sheep.

'They're called "cows" and kept in another big cage, in a different part of the island. They are locked up all the time and twice a day they are "milked" for the white liquid that comes from the big pouches that hang underneath their tummies.'

Juno knew what milk was, as she had been fed it by her humans when she was an abandoned puppy. She had not known where it came from before.

'Maybe you and I can do something for these cows? Just like you did for the chickens,' suggested the sheep.

'More mistreated animals!' exclaimed Juno. 'Of course we should do something.'

Ovinius baaahed his approval.

'Just don't send me the wrong way again,' Juno chided him.

Ovinius looked down and shook his head. 'I'll ask Walter for more information next time he trots past.'

57

As she walked back up the hill, Juno thought about this new rescue mission. If cows were as big as horses, it would be much more difficult than rescuing the chickens. She hoped there weren't 149 cows to rescue! It would also be difficult to find room for them at her house. They didn't belong in the chicken coop as they weren't chickens, and they sounded far too big to share her basket.

But first she had to talk to her sisters, Chester and Horatio. These poor cows needed help – they had another mission to plan!

CHAPTER 5

Juno and the Team Hoof It to the Cows

Juno spoke seriously to her sisters. They were having a pack conference under the big tree near the house.

'What I am about to tell you is in strict confidence.'

Jingles, the youngest, nodded and panted. Juniper's ears pricked up as they both listened to their leader.

'Ovinius has told me about more animals that need rescuing,' Juno explained. 'They are called cows, and are trapped in a shed like the chickens were. They have never felt the grass underneath their feet or been allowed outside. Will you help me?'

With a collective howl, which is what dog packs do when they are excited, they said yes!

'A long time ago, Ovinius told me about sheepdogs. Special types of dogs which herd sheep into pens, and they do it very well, without hurting the sheep. Do you think you could be "cow-dogs", a sort of sheepdog for cows? It was Ovinius' idea.'

A few days went by, with no news from Ovinius or Walter, so the dogs spent time with the chickens, who by now had all been given names.

'Although it took a lot longer than expected,' Gladys explained to Juno, beak in the air. 'Some of them were very choosy about it.'

Four days after the conference under the tree, Chester and Horatio hopped all the way up the hill.

'We have the directions to the cowshed!' they shouted, grins showing their buck teeth. 'Shall we go?'

Juno calmed the little rabbits down. 'There are things we need to know first.'

'Like what?' asked Chester.

'First, how far is the shed from the house? How

long it will take to get there? Where will the cows live? What do they eat?'

'Finding the shed is easy,' boasted Horatio. 'We've got Walter's directions. It's half an hour's hopping from the sheep field, in the opposite direction to the chicken shed.'

Thinking of a place for the cows to sleep was proving tricky. Juno had thought that some of them could sleep in the spare beds in the house, but there were only two of those and Juniper was reluctant to share her favourite sofa with a cow. They agreed, having never seen a cow, to get them home and then work something out.

The next morning, the group of well-rested and determined animals met in Ovinius' field. Juno's tail had been tingling since the moment she sneezed herself awake.

'Ready?' she asked them. Coming on the mission were Juno, Jingles, Chester and Horatio. Charles was providing air surveillance. Ovinius and Juniper were standing by at the house to help when the party returned home.

The journey to the cow shed was uneventful, as Walter's directions had been good and nobody had sent them the wrong way. The gang travelled in silence and covered ground quickly, Chester travelling part of the way on Juno's back, Horatio on Jingles'. Charles was already there, circling overhead and keeping a watchful eye. He gave a single caw to indicate that all was quiet.

The shed was smaller than the one that had held the chickens, and there was much less noise. Just some gentle grunting, which the animals would later learn were called "moos". The sun was only just peeping over the horizon and there was no sign of any farmer humans. Julia, an authority on bad farmers, had told them to arrive as early as possible.

The bunnies darted off to find an opening in the shed. Juno and Jingles crouched down behind some nearby trees. It seemed like an age before Chester and Horatio hopped back.

Chester updated them. 'The whole of the other side of the shed is just open. There's no wall at all, we'll have no trouble.'

'Walter the Horse was right,' continued Horatio.

'There are seven large animals inside. They have big black and white faces, big ears and pouches hanging under their tummies.'

'They're huge!' added Chester. 'And separated from each other by a big metal fence. They can see each other through the gaps, and also out into the yard outside, though they don't seem to have much room to turn around. There's some kind of sludge in troughs for them to eat, so you will have to go behind them to open the gate and let them out. The food smells horrible!'

Juno shuddered as she remembered barely being able to turn around in the hole. 'Thank you, bunnies,' she said. They had no time to waste, the sun was rising and the farmer humans would wake up soon.

As leader, Juno poked her head around the corner first, to check that it was safe. She approached on tip-paws so as not to frighten the cows. The others followed and soon they were in front of the seven big cows. The cows' eyes widened when they saw two dogs and two bunnies. 'We don't get many visitors,' they explained later.

'What are you doing here?' the biggest cow asked.

'We're here to help you escape,' announced Juno. 'Out of this horrible shed and to our house where you will have lots more room.'

'My name is Primrose, and I am the Head Cow,' the biggest cow replied. She looked around at the other cows. 'We have dreamed of being free in a field and not having to make so much milk.' She looked down through her big eyelashes. 'It is very painful.'

'There are lots of fields where we live,' said Juno, 'with really green grass.'

'Our cages all have latches at the back,' Primrose explained. 'They are quite easy to release from the outside. We've watched the farmer. We need to hurry, he won't like it if he finds us gone.'

As the expert in latches, Juno went behind the cows and used her snout to open Primrose's. It was a bit twistier than the one on her kitchen door, but once she figured that out the Head Cow was quickly free. Jingles watched Juno work, and quickly "latched", as usual, on to the plan.

The dogs got to work enthusiastically, and although the first two latches were a little bit difficult, within three minutes all the gates were open. The seven cows stood, uncertain. Primrose took charge.

'Right,' she bellowed. 'Let's move. We need to very carefully walk backwards. Violet, after me. Then Lynne, Willow, Hyacinth, Matilda, and Imelda, you go last.' Being the Head Cow, Primrose went first.

It was crowded in the shed with two big dogs, two rabbits and seven cows free of their pens. Now they needed to get away before their farmer could spot them.

'We need to go,' Juno commanded, as she heard Charles' loud and distinctive squawk. Twice. She felt the now-familiar tingle in her tail. 'Charles says something is wrong.' She crept closer to the yard and Charles flew down to meet her.

'The farmer's house is the one you walked past on the way. He's awake now, drinking tea in his kitchen.'

'But there's no other way off the farm!' protested Juno.

'Exactly,' replied Charles. He flew off to check on the farmer again.

How would Juno get seven cows past without the farmer seeing? If he saw them he would stop them, and maybe even punish the cows.

Juno thought for a moment and turned back to the waiting animals. 'Walk silently on the lawn in the front of the house, don't go on the cobbled path, even though it's quicker. The farmer would hear your hooves clattering.'

Placing their feet carefully on the still-wet grass, the cows left the shed for the first time. The sun was bright, so they blinked their eyes and relied on Juno, Jingles and the bunnies to direct them, running around the cows' feet like cow-dogs. The farmer guzzled tea and shovelled in his breakfast as his cows silently processed past his window.

Juno counted them as they reached the nearby forest. One, two, three-

'Caw! Caw!' screeched Charles. Juno watched, claws digging into the ground, as the farmer turned towards the window, four cows still left in his front garden.

'Ebenezer!' called a lady's voice from inside the house, and the farmer turned back, away from the window.

'Yikes! That was close,' thought Juno. Four, five, six cows had made it out of the garden.

'Caw! Caw!' shouted Charles again. The front door of the farmer's cottage was opening! Juno looked on helplessly as Jingles and the bunnies hurried Matilda on, and in the doorway the farmer began to turn.

'Holy cow!' he shouted as Charles swooped down. The bird flapped his big wings in the farmer's face, and the farmer threw his arms up to protect himself.

'Get off!' he shouted, and tried to get back into his cottage. 'Get off!'

The cows rounded the corner into the forest and onto the path that would lead them to Juno's home. Walter had directed them this way to avoid cars. They trotted along at high speed, but Juno still kept a close watch.

Ovinius was there to welcome them as they neared the house, waving hello with a hoof. The humans arrived home from walking Juniper, just as Juno was trying to nudge Primrose through the back door. Their mouths fell open and they gaped at the procession of dogs and cows.

'What on earth ... Where did you get these from?' asked the man human.

'Juno! They can't stay here,' the lady one told her.

Juno whined. She hadn't got the cows all the way back home to have to find somewhere else for

them to live.

'Let's put them in with the sheep,' the female human continued. 'The field is big enough.'
Juno touched her face with her paw. She should have thought of that.

'And we'll have to work out what to do with ... one, three, SEVEN cows,' added the male one, in a weary voice. 'Juno, are you trying to build your own ark?'

CHAPTER 6

Happy as a Muddy Piggy

Juno was a little late for her morning walk as she treated herself to a lie in after the cow rescue. Gladys was still in her usual place when the Top Dog arrived at the coop.

'Let me know how the cows are,' Gladys said. 'The chickens are longing to meet them.'

As Juno ambled down the hill to Ovinius' much busier field, the cows stopped chewing the grass and let out an enormous grunt of appreciation.

'How are you all doing?' asked Juno.

'Very well,' answered Ovinius. 'It's very good grass here.'

'I was asking the cows,' said Juno.

Primrose was delighted to see her. 'Ovinius is right,' she agreed. 'There's plenty of room to roam, the grass is good and there's lots of fresh water to drink.'

'The vet came,' added Ovinius, as if he had arranged this. The vet had rubbed ointment on the cows' pouches to make them feel better. Being milked all the time made them very sore!

'It's all thanks to you Juno. We will never forget what you did for us,' Primrose said. Juno bowed her head.

'It was my plan that saved you,' Ovinius chimed in. 'The cow-dog plan. It was my idea.'

Juno ignored him, he was irredeemable. 'What was it like?' she asked Primrose. 'In the shed?'

Primrose's big dark eyes moistened, and a big tear rolled down her face. Juno nuzzled up against the cow's flank to reassure her and said, 'I didn't mean to upset you.'

'We were kept in the shed almost from the beginning,' said Primrose. 'Separate from each other. We could talk, but not nuzzle each other or even go for a walk. I made us all keep fit by marching on the spot. I wanted to be in the world beyond the shed.' She looked at the field she was in now, with its green grass and view of forest and hills. 'We could see it from our pens. We had to have calves all the time, as if we didn't have babies we wouldn't make any milk. And that's what the farmer wants, you know. Milk.'

Milk from cows was apparently drunk by humans, and indeed Juno had seen her humans put this milk in their cups of tea. The cows, however, were fed a sort of liquid sludge, as the rabbits had noticed. The farmer would put big sucking machines on the pouches – Primrose explained these were called udders – underneath the cows' tummies. This was what could be so painful and why the vet had given them ointment, as sometimes the machine didn't fit right. They were milked twice a day, even on their birthdays!

'The worst part,' Primrose continued, 'is when new calves are born. They are always taken away and we don't know what happens to them. Our babies.'

Willow sniffed. 'We always think about them and hope they are OK.'

Juno said nothing and nuzzled Willow. She thought that these poor calves were probably not OK. She also said nothing when Primrose

mentioned that older cows who didn't make as much milk were taken away never to be seen again.

Sheep, dogs, horses and cats lived much longer than three or four years, and Juno thought that probably cows would as well. She told Primrose about the chickens she had rescued and how they had been forced to lay eggs every day. 'I hope there are no more animals that are treated badly, like you and the chickens.'

'I saw the farmer with a different kind of animal once,' Primrose answered. 'When I was looking out of my pen. Pink ones. A bit bigger than you.'

'Pink dogs? I've never heard of pink dogs,' said Juno.

'These weren't dogs,' insisted Primrose. 'They had little curly tails and big, odd-looking snouts. They were only in the yard outside the shed for a little while and the farmer was with them. They made funny squealing noises.'

Juno wanted to find these funny animals. If Primrose's horrible farmer was with them, they would need her help.

CHAPTER 7

This Little Piggy Won't Go to Market

That night, Juno tossed and turned in her big basket. The next day, she accidentally spilled some of her water and trod on Juniper's tail. She was thinking about the pink animals.

On her morning walk she saw Charles. 'Charles, will you meet me over by the big tree so that we can talk in private?' she asked him.

Charles half-flew and half-walked there in his funny crow way. Juno told him what she had heard about the pink animals and asked if he had seen anything like that.

'No, but I can fly round the island and look,' Charles said. 'If a farmer has them, they are here somewhere.'

'Primrose said they make a squealing sound,' Juno told him as much as she could about the new animal.

Charles spread his big shiny wings, gave Juno
a wink with one of his beady yellow eyes, and flew
off.

He returned when Juno was checking on Gladys and the chickens, the sun was low in the sky. Charles landed in front of her and spoke in a low voice. 'I've found something, but it's not good news.'

'Go on,' urged Juno, moving away from the chickens so they couldn't overhear.

'I was near the middle of the island when I saw something glinting in an abandoned field. Sure enough it was a gloomy shed, about the same size as the cow's one. It squealed, just like you said.'

'Did you look inside?' panted Juno.

'I found a hole in the roof. It was very dark inside, but I could make out about six big animals and seven baby ones. I whispered to them and asked if they could tell me what was going on.' Charles scratched his beak with his foot. 'The biggest one, who is very big indeed, said they were called pigs and needed help.'

'I knew it!' breathed Juno.

'The shed smelled awful, muck everywhere. The biggest pig said her name was Ella, and that every few months the farmer would talk to his helper about something called a "market" and that half the big pigs would be taken away, never to return.'

'Just like the cows!' thought Juno.

'I told Ella that my friend Juno is coming to rescue her, just like she rescued the cows and chickens.'

And indeed Juno was. The next day, she assembled her rescue crew in a clearing near the pig shed.

'If we don't rescue the pigs,' she explained, 'they might never be seen again, like Primrose's friends. We must remain focused.'

As she said it, she gave a pointed look to some of the more excitable animals, Jingles and Chester in particular, and Gladys and Julia who were on Walter's back. The horse, chickens and even Primrose hadn't wanted to miss out on this adventure.

Chester and Horatio checked out the shed first, and – through a grille in the wall – warned Ella, that Juno and the others were coming.

Immediately, the pigs stopped squealing, and the mother pig gathered her seven little piglets to her side, saying, 'Piglets, you need to be quiet for Mummy, and you have to do everything I tell you. It is very, very important.'

The other animals heard the squealing stop, and Juno said, 'Time to take up your positions. Walter, Gladys, Julia, Juniper, and Primrose, keep your eyes peeled.' They were lookouts, sent to keep watch all around the shed so the farmer couldn't surprise them.

'Jingles, Chester, Horatio, let's go!' Crouching low, the four animals silently made their way to the shed. Juno looked carefully at the door and saw that the latch had a kind of metal spike sticking out of a small hole. She had seen her humans turn those kinds of spikes at night, when they were closing the doors to the house.

'I will try and use my teeth on the metal spike,' said Juno to Chester, as her paws couldn't quite turn it.

'Wait,' he said, as he had spotted something just next to the yard. It was a little piece of cloth, like the cloth used for the dogs' coats when it was cold. 'Wrap the metal spike in the cloth, then, when you turn it with your mouth, you won't hurt yourself.'

'You brilliant little bunnies,' replied Juno, as she watched them jump up on Jingle's back so that they could reach the spike and wrap the cloth around it. Juno carefully put her mouth and teeth over, and, with quite an effort, managed to turn the spike. The door opened!

The shed was gloomy and dirty. The poor pigs, unused to light, blinked as the sunlight streamed in.

'We are here to rescue you and take you to our house,' announced Juno. 'Don't be frightened.'

As she spoke there was a terrible squawking from outside the shed and Charles flew inside.

'Charles!' gasped Juno. 'What is it?'

'The bad farmer is sitting on a big red machine,' he cawed. 'He's pulling something behind it.' Charles paused for breath. 'It looks like a big cage.'

'Market,' breathed Juno. 'He's going to take them to market.' Her tail was fizzing so much it was almost painful. 'Tell the others to distract him.' Charles flew back outside the shed. By now Juno and the pigs could hear the motor of the farmer's tractor, and the pigs started to squeal.

'You're too late!' wailed Ella.

Walter had other ideas. He trotted nearer to the tractor, Gladys and Julia squawked loudly and flapped their wings from their position on the horse's back. Primrose, meanwhile, was indicating to the pigs that they should follow her out of the building.

'Get out of my way!' the farmer shouted at Walter, Gladys and Julia. In the corner of his eye, Walter spotted something. He got out of the way.

'That's better,' said the farmer. 'Hold on a minute, what are you doing? Stop it now!'

Walter had spotted a wooden log near the tractor, and he rolled it with his big horse's head right into the path of the machine.

The log of wood stopped the machine. The farmer shouted and got off the tractor to move the log, as it had got stuck in the front wheels.

The dogs, bunnies, pigs and cow ran at top speed away from the shed, away from the farmer and towards Juno's house.

The farmer got the log away, and huffing and puffing, got back onto his machine and headed for the shed, which by now was empty.

'Oh yes,' he muttered to himself. 'I'll find you piggies alright.'

He knew all the ways out of his farm, and made a lucky guess that the pigs would be on the very path they were on. He found trotter prints and followed them.

Charles was the one who noticed first. 'Quick!'

he screeched. 'You must be faster. The farmer is coming.'

'Ovinius!' Primrose shouted as the sheep field came into sight. 'Gather your flock, as well as my herd, and come onto the path.'

When the farmer arrived at Ovinius' field, he almost ran into a crowd of sheep and cows blocking his way. The animals glared at him, and he watched helplessly as 'his' pigs headed towards Juno's house halfway up the hill.

'I'll get you back,' he yelled as he turned and left.

'Hooray!' cheered the animals. 'We did it!'

Juno was not so sure the farmer was beaten.

'Let's stop here,' said Ella. They were halfway up the hill. 'It's a lovely view.'

'I think we should find my humans,' said Juno. 'You'll be safe then.'

'Humans!' exclaimed Ella. 'We don't need more of those. We want to enjoy being free.' She closed her piggy eyes and breathed in. The rest of the herd followed her example.

Juno's humans were not far away, having a cup of tea outside the house, as they did every evening. If the pigs would not go to them, Juno would bring them to the pigs. She padded up to the house and offered her head to be patted.

'What is it, Juno?' the man human said, when Juno took his shirt in her mouth and tried to drag him up from his chair and towards the pigs. His face drained of colour when he looked down the hill. 'You'll never believe this ...' he said to the lady one.

'More animals! Juno, we can't fit any more animals in, where will they live?' the lady human cried. 'Juno, we can't this time. This is enough.'

'Oh no!' thought Juno.

Two humans and a dog looked up at the loud sound of a machine. It was the bad farmer on his tractor with the cage on the back. He drew to a stop on the driveway and got out, red-faced and spluttering.

'My pigs!' he shouted. At the sound of his voice the pigs stood up and started to squeal. 'How dare you! They're mine and they're due at market first thing tomorrow! I don't know how you trained this dog to steal them, but I'm taking them back.' He rolled up his sleeves.

Juno's humans were both standing now. The man one said, 'assuming they are your pigs, they're here now and don't seem to want to go back with you!'

'How much money do you want?' asked the lady human. 'For all of them.' The other human looked at her in surprise.

Juno remembered what "money" was, as Jingles, when she was a little puppy, had chewed some bits of paper, and been told off by the humans. These bits of paper were very important to the humans.

They also seemed very valuable to the farmer. He stopped shouting and thought. 'One hundred,' he said after a few moments. 'To compensate for the loss of my sausages...'

'OK,' the lady human said immediately and handed over money from her purse.

The Farmer snorted, got back on the tractor and drove away. The humans turned to Juno. *Thank you*, she said in her own way, licking their hands.

'The pigs can stay in the forest over there,' said the male human, patting her affectionately. 'But your ark is big enough now. No more animals!'

CHAPTER 8

The Shiny Spoons of Happiness

The pigs settled in the forest next to Juno's house, and every day they got the scraps from the humans' meals, and also extra vegetables from a neighbour's garden. The chickens were laying eggs, but only when they wanted to, and they didn't mind the humans having the eggs for breakfast now they had space as well as tasty food. Their feathers were sleek and glossy, and there were in fact so many eggs that the humans were able to get "money" for them. The cows and the sheep mingled happily in Ovinius' field where Juno, Jingles and Juniper often visited them.

One morning, the humans called the dogs over to get in the car to go for a walk somewhere new.

Juno, Jingles and Juniper loved going on walks, especially in new and interesting places. On the way the humans spoke to Juno.

'Juno, we know you love animals,' said the man, who was driving, 'and that you don't want them to suffer. But we just can't fit any more in our house.'

'A friend of ours has a new type of farm,' continued the lady, 'which makes meat, eggs and milk exactly the same as pigs, chickens and cows make, but without any animals suffering!'

'Without any animals at all, in fact,' added the man as he turned the car left down a country lane. 'And we're going to show it to you.'

Juno was familiar with almost all of the island after her recent adventures, but she didn't recognise this road. Her tail tingled. When the car stopped, the dogs all piled out, though Juniper had to be helped a bit.

'This is the new type of farm,' announced the humans. 'It's more of a factory really, a place where things are made efficiently... Shall we go?'

Juniper was quite content to walk alongside the humans, but Juno and Jingles bounded off to have a good look at the big shiny shed ahead of them. There were whirring noises coming from it, but no squealing or squawking. Some new humans – one with hair the colour of straw, and one with a big nose – greeted Juno's humans enthusiastically, then turned to the dogs. Jingles bounded up to them, wagging her tail and licking their hands, which the new humans seemed to like. Juno was more reserved, but still friendly.

'Good Dog,' they said to her when they patted her head, which the dogs had noticed was about all that most humans (but not theirs!) said to them. Juno suspected they thought that dogs don't have a wide vocabulary – they were very wrong about that!

While Jingles was being made a fuss of, Juno slipped inside the factory to have a quick look. Her humans had said there were no unhappy animals here, but Juno was experienced in farms now and wanted to check it out for herself.

There were lots of big containers with what looked like giant shiny spoons going round and round inside of them, and indeed, no animals.

Juno knew what a spoon was because that was used to measure out the dogs' dinners. Maybe this was stirring the food, Juno speculated, although she couldn't see any. She went round a corner and growled.

It was the bad pig farmer! What was he doing here?

She raced back to Jingles and the humans. 'The bad farmer is here!' she barked. Where he was, unhappy animals would not be far away.

'What's wrong, Juno?' asked her man human.

She barked in response and started running. *Come this way!* All the humans – Juno's, and the new ones – followed her to where the new farmer was looking at the spoons. Juno stood in front of him, as if to say 'see!'

The farmer gave a start, before smiling and continuing on his way. The lady human patted Juno reassuringly. Juno looked up at her, questioning. This was the bad farmer! Didn't they remember? 'That's Ebenezer,' explained one of the factory-owning humans. 'He got a job here after his farm closed. He works very hard, we're lucky to have him.' Jingles licked his hand again. 'Your dogs are so affectionate! How do they know Ebenezer? Juno didn't like him much!'

If my humans are OK with him, thought Juno, then he must have changed. Like Ovinius.

Juno and Jingles straightened up, proud that

the new humans were so positive about them. Their humans laughed. 'Juno has been rescuing caged farmed animals, including Ebenezer's pigs. We have quite the menagerie at home. We call it Juno's Ark!'

'How did that happen?'

Juno's humans explained about coming home and finding Julia one day, 149 new chickens the next. Then cows, then pigs. 'Ebenezer wasn't very happy with us, but we did give him money for the pigs.'

The new humans laughed and laughed. 'So this is the famous dog!' they said. 'We didn't quite believe Ebenezer when he told us a dog had stolen all his animals.'

'We really can't fit any more animals in the house, so we brought Juno here.'

'I see!' said the one with hair like straw. 'Well, Juno, let me tell you a bit more. We don't believe that any animals should suffer because humans want to drink milk and eat sausages, so we worked out a way of growing milk, meat and eggs instead.'

'It sounds like something from a science fiction novel!' exclaimed Juno's man human.

'We take a tiny sample of cells from each of the animals,' continued the human with the big nose. 'This doesn't hurt them at all, but, thanks to science, we can use the sample to grow the bits of the cow, or pig, or chicken that we want. We only grow the edible bits.'

'Just fat and muscle?'

The other factory human nodded. 'Yes, that's it. No feathers, fur, udders, horns or hooves here! No waste, and much less pollution than there is from growing animals.'

'See, Juno!' said her lady human, patting her on the head. 'No more suffering for animals like your friends. The food that used to come from animals can be made without them.'

Juno wagged her tail. With factories like this one, Primrose, Julia, Ella and animals like them wouldn't have to live in cramped horrible sheds and live miserable and short lives.

Just then Ebenezer, the former farmer, appeared with three bowls of what looked like chicken.

'Chicken from the factory,' he announced proudly, and put the bowls in front of the dogs to

try. It looked like chicken. It smelled like chicken. Juniper dove in, smacking her lips, Jingles not far behind.

'It tastes exactly like chicken. It's delicious,' sighed Juniper.

'Hurry up or I'll eat yours,' Jingles told Juno.

Juno's tail tingled and she realised she wanted more than just cruelty-free meat. She had a taste for adventure now, and she wondered what would come next.

ACKNOWLEDGEMENTS

Woofs, Treats and Wags to everyone who helped with this book.

First big Bow-Wow to Lauren Mitchell, who has done an amazing job editing and putting the project together. Without her, *Juno's Ark* would still be in my head.

Then to Trish, my sister and right-hand woman, a huge paw in her direction, as she has been similarly indispensable.

Our brilliant illustrator Simone Fumagalli has brought Juno and her friends to life.

To our designer Sophie Stericker, who has made *Juno's Ark* into a real book.

Dafina, the Mother of Hounds and my dear darling girl, inventor of the title of the book as well as editor.

And of course, to James the Cat, and to the real life wonderful dogs, in particular to our heroine, Juno, who is working on our next book already!

HOW JIM MET JUNO

The real Juno started her life in a horrid way, in a cage, in one of the most disgraceful animal dog shelters on the planet. Her mother, Juniper, who now lives with Juno and Jim, was probably forced to have pups, despite being fragile and small.

Jim and his partner adopted Juniper and her puppies, but were only able to bring Juno and her siblings back to her loving home when she was eight weeks old. In this time Juniper escaped from the shelter. The dogs there were chained up, badly fed, and lived in horrible conditions.

While Juno and her siblings got to know Jim, Juniper got to know Ibiza. It wasn't until three years later, Juniper roaming all around the island in the meantime, that Jim was able to welcome her into his home, where she has been happy ever since.

Today, Juno, Juniper, Jingles, Twisis, Rey, Circles and Bowie – all of them special characters – live together, play together, and bring Jim and his partner the greatest joy imaginable.

Jim lives with his partner, their seven dogs (one of whom is the real Juno) and twelve chickens on not just one, but two islands. The islands are quite different, as Ibiza is generally hot and the Isle of Man is rain-lashed, but they are both beautiful.

Jim went to school and university in England, where he majored in economics and politics. He has been working for a long time, in all sorts of industries, but in the past twenty years or so has become passionate about the health of humanity and, more recently, changing the food system to be kinder to animals and the environment.

Jim has written or co-written eight books about investment and industry, *Juno's Ark* is his first work of fiction.

He enjoyed writing this one much more than any of the others.

CELL-EBRATING CELLS!

At the end of the story, when Juno, Jingles and Juniper were taken to the shiny new factory where they sampled the delicious chicken, they tried food made by what scientists call "cellular agriculture".

This is a fancy term for making meat, fish, cocoa and cotton (as well as other materials like leather) in a way that doesn't kill or hurt animals.

Every living thing on earth – including us – is made up of billions and trillions of tiny little things called cells. These are too small to see without a microscope, but they are in a permanent state of motion. Dividing, growing, and doing lots of things in our bodies that keep us healthy. It's the same for all animals and plants.

Some special types of cells are known as stem cells, because they are the ones from which all the other types of cells grow – these include our hearts, hair, bones, brains and skin. They are really important, and over the years, clever scientists have worked out a way to take a few of these cells from animals, fish and plants and make them grow in big stainless steel vats called bioreactors.

The cells that scientists can produce from these tiny samples are the ones that are really useful to produce food. So, for instance the cells that make scales on fish, or horns on cows are not used, but only the ones that produce the nutritious parts, the fat and muscle, which are the main ingredients of the meat and fish we eat.

After about six weeks of being fed things like starch and sugars, these cells from the tiny sample can produce a whole lot of meat, or fish, or coffee, or almost anything we want. This will one day be cheaper than growing these foods on regular farms. The impact on the environment is minimal compared to normal farming, meaning that producing meat this way will also help fight climate change.

Most importantly for Juno, no animals are hurt.

In a few years, lots of dogs and humans will be eating food made in this way, and drinking milk and eating ice cream made in a slightly different way (precision fermentation). Animals like Gladys, Primrose and Ella can live out their lives in peace and happiness.

No wonder Juno was so excited about what she saw – and tasted – at the shiny new factory. This really is something to CELL-ebrate!!

JUNO'S SUPPORT

Sales of this book will be donated to two charities close to Jim's heart, *Compassion in World Farming* and a shelter specifically for podenco dogs near his home in Ibiza.

Compassion in World Farming is the leading farm animal welfare charity, campaigning peacefully to end factory farming and create a better future for all farm animals.

You can find more about them on their website www.ciwf.org.uk

DUO, which stands for Danos una Oportunidad (Give us a Chance) is a dog shelter for abandoned and mistreated dogs located in Ibiza, Spain. It currently houses 35 dogs of all breeds - and many Ibizan hounds just like Juno - who are waiting to find their forever home. We hope that you can give them a chance so that they can help more dogs like Juno.

Find out more about them on their Instagram page

duo_ibiza_animal_rescue

PUZZLES

1.
149 chickens is a lot to name, can you think of a name for every letter of the alphabet like Gladys did?

2.
If an Ibizan Podenco can run at 40km per hour, how long does it take Juno to run 4km?

3.
If she can walk at 5km per hour, how long does it take for her to walk 10km?

5.
If the average dairy cow weighs 500kg, how much does Juno's herd weigh?

4.
If every hen in the coop (the 150 rescued hens as well as Gladys and her original flock of 10) has 5 square meters of space, how big is the whole coop?

6.
How much better do you think Juno is able to smell than humans?

Answers on the next page

ANSWERS

1. The names are up to you!
   You need 26

2. 6 minutes

3. 2 hours

4. The coop is 805 square meters big

5. With seven cows in Juno's herd,
   they would weigh around 3,500kg

6. Dogs can smell between 10,000
   and 100,000 times better than
   humans

FIND JUNO

Can you find Juno and her friends hiding in the wordsearch?

B	S	O	V	E	E	G	C	H
J	U	L	I	A	K	L	H	O
U	U	F	U	R	I	A	L	R
N	L	N	J	K	S	D	F	A
O	G	X	I	H	N	Y	M	T
M	I	B	N	P	R	S	Q	I
Q	E	S	G	H	E	J	H	O
H	W	A	L	T	E	R	I	J
J	U	Q	E	S	P	A	F	S
L	B	E	S	K	W	S	A	L

JUNO   JULIA   GLADYS   JUNIPER
JINGLES   HORATIO   ELLA   WALTER

Answers on the next page

FIND JUNO
- ANSWERS

B	S	O	V	E	E	G	C	H
J	U	L	I	A	K	L	H	O
U	U	F	U	R	I	A	L	R
N	L	N	J	K	S	D	F	A
O	G	X	I	H	N	Y	M	T
M	I	B	N	P	R	S	Q	I
Q	E	S	G	H	E	J	H	O
H	W	A	L	T	E	R	I	J
J	U	Q	E	S	P	A	F	S
L	B	E	S	K	W	S	A	L

Did you find the extra word?